Daffodil
and the
Birthday Surprise

Fulton Books, Inc.
Meadville, PA

Published by Fulton Books 2021

ISBN 978-1-64952-362-4 (paperback)
ISBN 978-1-64952-363-1 (digital)

Printed in the United States of America

Daffodil
and the
Birthday Surprise

Mindy Melton

"One, two, three! Okay, open them," her mom said.

Opening her eyes, Daffodil stared at the most beautiful pink dress she'd ever seen. "I love it! It's the most perfect birthday dress ever!" Daffodil said excitedly. She couldn't wait to show her best friend, Rosie.

"I thought it went great with your hair," her mom said, smiling.

She's right. It does go great with her hair! You see, Daffodil was quite unique. She was born with rainbow-colored hair.

Magic rainbow-colored hair to be exact.

Sitting on her bed, Daffodil called Rosie.

"It's so pretty, Rosie! It's pink and sparkly and has a big ribbon on the front," Daffodil said happily.

"I can't wait to see it. Can you ask your mom if you can come over? I have a birthday gift for you too," Rosie said.

With her mom's approval, Daffodil set off to Rosie's house in her new pink dress.

Happily on her way, she saw her friend Bird. Bird looked to be struggling with a big pile of ribbons.

"What's the matter, Bird?" asked Daffodil.

"I'm having trouble tying these ribbons into bows. They keep getting tangled," Bird replied.

"I'd love to help you!"

With a twist and twirl of her red hair, Daffodil untangled Bird's ribbons.

"Thank you, Daffodil!" Bird said gratefully. "Now I can make my bows."

As Daffodil continued on her walk, she got a whiff of something that smelled sweet and delicious. Up ahead, she spotted Unicorn's house.

"Hi, Unicorn, what's that sweet smell?" she asked.

"I'm trying to make chocolate ice cream, but something is missing. I just can't seem to get it right," replied Unicorn.

"I can help you with that. Mind if I have a taste?" asked Daffodil.

Just then, she knew just what it needed! With a twist and twirl of her orange hair, Unicorn now had a heaping bucket full of rich, creamy, chocolate ice cream.

"Oh, thank you! Thank you!" exclaimed Unicorn.

"Enjoy!" Daffodil smiled.

Just then, she heard someone crying. She came across her friend Butterfly.

"What's the matter, Butterfly?" asked Daffodil.

"My meadow has no flowers," she cried.

"Don't worry, I can help your meadow bloom bright, beautiful flowers of every color."

With a twist and twirl of her yellow hair, the meadow was filled with hundreds of colorful flowers.

"Oh, thank you so much, Daffodil!"

With a nod, Daffodil continued on her way.

Just as she was about to pass the den of her friend Bear, she heard a loud *grrrr*. Startled, Daffodil stopped to check on him.

"Whatcha doin', Bear?" she asked.

"I need green paint, but the only color I have is white," he said, a bit frustrated.

"Maybe I can help you?" Daffodil suggested.

With a twist and twirl of her green hair, Daffodil made a vibrant green paint for Bear.

"*Wow!*" exclaimed Bear. "Just the color I needed! Thanks, Daffodil," Bear said gratefully.

With a wave, she set off to Rosie's house.

In the distance, Daffodil heard a very loud roar. Concerned, she moved toward the sound to find her friend Tiger.

"Tiger, are you all right?!" Daffodil questioned.

"Well, no, I'm low on sugar. I don't have enough for what my recipe calls for," he stressed.

"I can help you get more sugar for your recipe. Watch this!"

With a twist and twirl of her blue hair, Daffodil made a big sack of sugar for Tiger.

"Wooh! That's more than enough for my recipe. Thank you, Daffodil," Tiger said excitedly.

With a wink, Daffodil skipped away.

ROOAARRR!!"

Just then, she saw a big cloud of smoke up ahead. She hurried over to see what it was and found her friend Dragon.

"Dragon, is everything okay?" she asked.

"I'm trying to make candles, but I can't seem to get them to form."

"Well, I can make you candles if you'd like," she said calmly.

"You can do that?" Dragon questioned.

"As a matter of fact, I can," Daffodil said confidently.

With a twist and twirl of her **purple** hair, Dragon now had a set of candles.

"These candles are perfect and just what I need! Thanks, Daffodil."

With that, she gave a little bob of her head and continued on her way.

Daffodil decided to take a break under a big shade tree. She thought long and hard about her friends and the way she helped them. It made her happy knowing she was able to do something nice for them. Smiling to herself, she was excited to tell Rosie all about the things that happened while walking to her house.

Finally arriving, she knocked on the door to Rosie's small cottage.

"COME IN!" yelled Rosie.

Daffodil opened the door and...

SURPRISE!!!

Startled, she saw all her friends: Bird, Unicorn, Butterfly, Bear, Tiger, and Dragon. They were all there.

"Happy birthday, Daffodil!" they all yelled.

23

"I brought birthday hats and tied them with the ribbons you helped me untangle," Bird said.

"I brought the creamy chocolate ice cream," said Unicorn.

"The flowers are from my meadow," replied Butterfly.

"I made the birthday banner with the green paint you helped make," grinned Bear.

"The sugar was just what I needed to make your cake," mentioned Tiger.

"And now it's time to make a wish and blow out your candles." Dragon smiled.

As Daffodil looked at her friends, she realized her wish already came true. With friends like hers, she already had everything she needed.

Well, except cake–she needed a piece of cake!

Happy Birthday Daffodil!

About the Author

Mindy Melton is a wife and mama to her two handsome boys. Every night before bed, her youngest son asks, "Can you tell me a story from your brain?" So that's exactly what she does. Her love of books and imagination have made some very fun stories. Living in sunny San Diego with her family, she loves spending time outside, riding bikes at the beach, going to the desert, and going on family camping trips. Coffee is an addiction, chocolate is a craving, and books are a passion. *Daffodil and the Birthday Surprise* is the first book in the Daffodil series.

CPSIA information can be obtained
at www.ICGtesting.com
Printed in the USA
LVHW060335080621
689674LV00005B/143